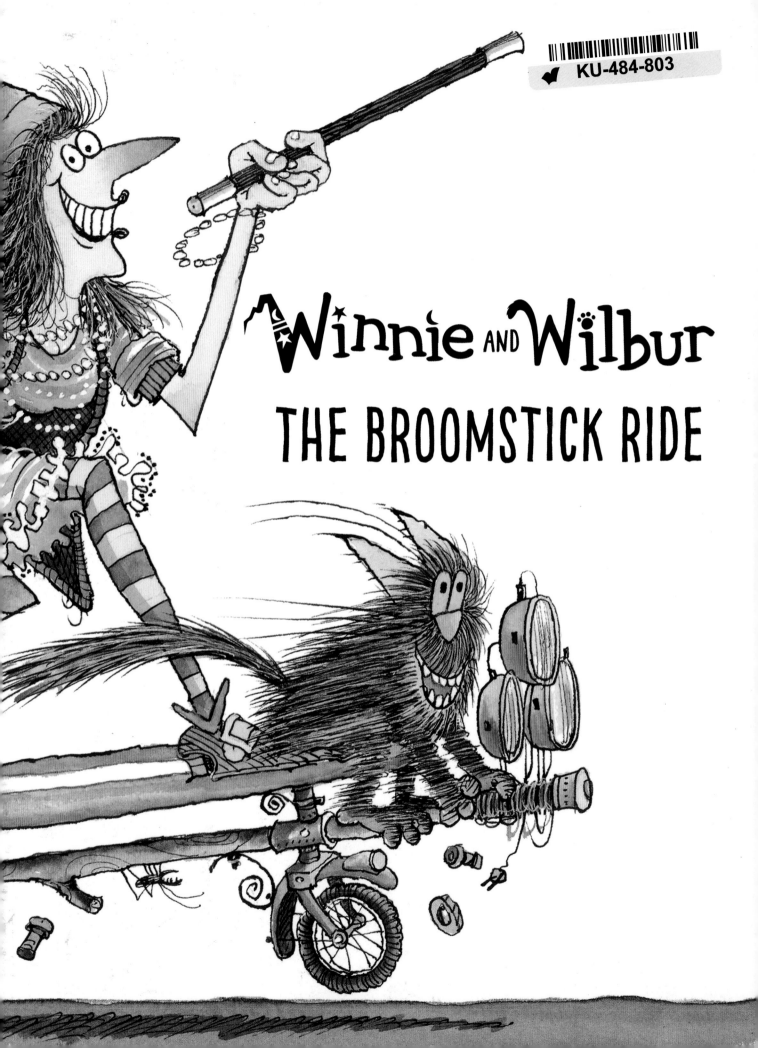

Winnie AND Wilbur
THE BROOMSTICK RIDE

Winnie the Witch always travelled by broomstick.
It was a wonderful way to travel.

Winnie would jump onto her broomstick.
Wilbur would jump onto her shoulder.
And they would zoom up into the sky.

There were no traffic lights.
No traffic jams.

Just the empty sky.

VALERIE THOMAS AND KORKY PAUL

Winnie AND Wilbur
UP, UP AND AWAY

Winnie AND Wilbur: THE BROOMSTICK RIDE

Winnie AND Wilbur: THE FLYING CARPET

Winnie AND Wilbur: THE AMAZING PUMPKIN

OXFORD
UNIVERSITY PRESS

Well, that was how it used to be.
But, just lately, the sky had become
rather crowded.

Last week, Winnie didn't see a helicopter.
Wilbur lost two of his whiskers.

The week before that,
she didn't see a hang glider.

Wilbur's tail was bent.

The week before that, a very tall
building suddenly got in her way.

Wilbur lost a clump of fur.

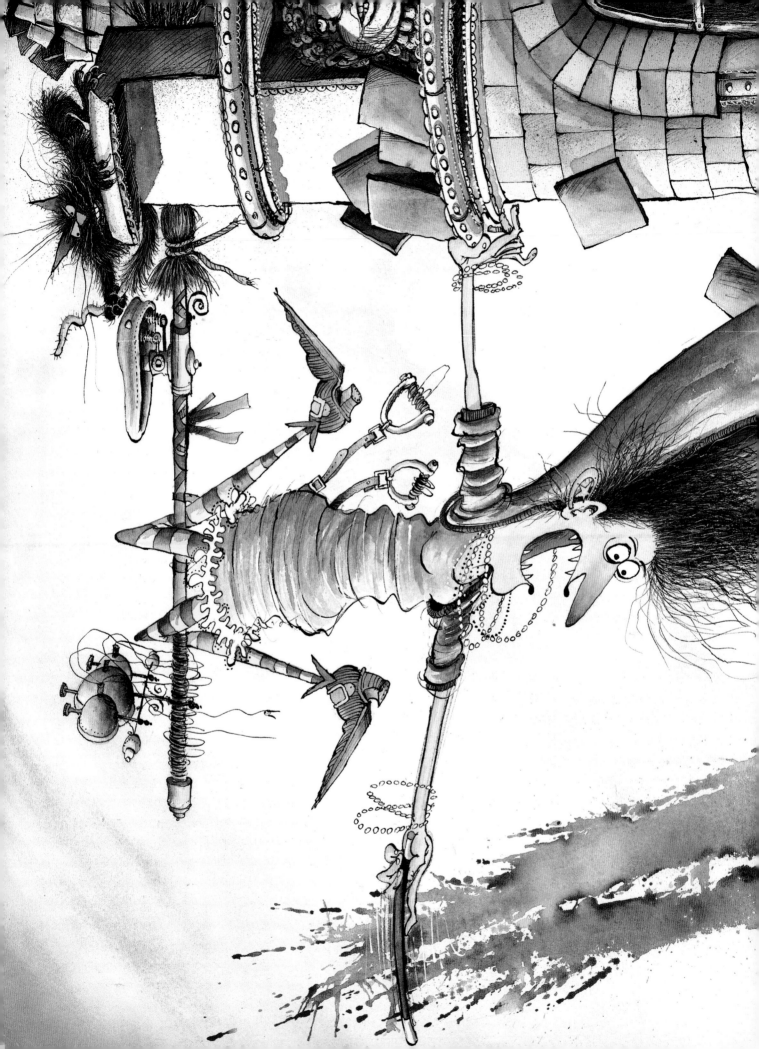

'The sky is too dangerous, Wilbur,' said Winnie.
'We'll have to try something else.'
So she took out her wand, waved it, and shouted,
'Abracadabra!'

Her broomstick turned into a
bicycle. But it was very slow.
Very hard to pedal.

And then a pond got in Winnie's way.
'She should look where she's going,' croaked a frog.

'A bicycle is worse than a broomstick, Wilbur,' said Winnie.
'We'll have to try something else.'
So she took out her wand, waved it, and shouted,

'Abracadabra!'

Her bicycle turned into a skateboard.
The skateboard was fast.
But it was hard to steer.
And impossible to stop.

Winnie was stopped. By an ice-cream seller.
'Can't you see where you're going?' he shouted.

'A skateboard is worse than a bicycle, Wilbur,' said Winnie.
'We'll have to try something else.'
So she took out her wand, waved it, and shouted,

'Abracadabra!'

Her skateboard turned into a horse,
and they trotted slowly down the path.
'This is much better than bicycles
or skateboards,' said Winnie.

But she didn't see . . .

. . . the low branch of a tree.
This time, Winnie didn't say anything.
She was hanging from a branch.

Slowly and carefully,
Winnie climbed down
from the tree.

'I think we'll walk
home, Wilbur,'
said Winnie.

They limped slowly along the road.
It was a very, very slow way to travel.

But it was safe.

Until Winnie stepped into a hole
and tumbled deep down under the ground.

YES WERE OPEN

'I think I need a
cup of tea,' Winnie said.

Winnie climbed out of the tunnel
and went into a shop.

'A cup of tea and a muffin, please,' she said.
'And a saucer of milk for my cat.'

'We don't sell cups of tea or muffins,'
said the shop lady.
'And we don't have saucers of milk.
But I think I can help you.'

And she sold Winnie a pair of spectacles.

Now, Winnie and Wilbur travel everywhere by broomstick.
It's a wonderful way to travel.

Winnie AND Wilbur
THE FLYING CARPET

Winnie the Witch was busy
writing letters.

They were thank-you letters
for her birthday presents.

Now there was only one left, the trickiest letter.
Winnie's sisters, Wilma, Wanda, and Wendy,
had given her a flying carpet.
Winnie had always wanted a flying carpet.
But *this* flying carpet had been a disappointment.

Actually, it had been a disaster.

Dear Wilma,

Wanda, and Wendy,

thank you very much

for the

There was the time it got tangled
in Winnie's washing.

And the day it tipped over as
they were passing a duck pond.

And then one day it turned a corner too quickly.

After that, Winnie rolled up the carpet, tied it with string . . .

put it in the broom cupboard, and locked the door.

But Winnie wanted to write something *nice*
about the carpet in her thank-you letter.

She unlocked the cupboard, untied the
carpet, and spread it on the armchair.

It is a beautiful carpet, she thought.
It seems a pity not to use it.

So Winnie decided to give it one
more chance.

Just then, the door bell rang.

Ding! Dong!

Winnie hurried off to answer it . . .

just as Wilbur came inside.

After a busy morning climbing trees
and chasing butterflies, he was ready
for a sleep.

The sun was shining on the flying carpet.
It looked so warm and comfortable.
Wilbur jumped up and in one minute
he was snoring.

The flying carpet waited
one more minute.

Then it rose gently into the air.
Wilbur didn't wake up.

It flew gently around the room.
Wilbur didn't wake up.

Mwah

Xelsy

MATILDA SNOOK

Then it zoomed out of the window.
Wilbur woke up.

'Meeoow!' he cried.

Winnie heard him.
She looked up, just in time to see the
flying carpet zoom up into the sky.

'Oh no!' cried Winnie. She grabbed her magic
wand and her broomstick, and zoomed up
into the sky after them.

Winnie flew as fast as her broomstick
could go, but the carpet was faster.
It swooped over the clock tower,
and under a bridge.

Winnie followed it.
'Hang on tight, Wilbur!' she called.

'Meeoow!' cried Wilbur.

Then the carpet flew over a funfair.
What fun!

First it whizzed down the
Roller Coaster Rocket.
Winnie whizzed down behind it.

Then it tried the
Terrible Twister.

The flying carpet was
having a wonderful time.
Wilbur was having a
horrible time.

Winnie was worried.
She would never catch them.

Then she had an idea.
She waved her magic wand,
shouted,

'Abracadabra!'

. . . and everything stopped.

Nothing whizzed or zoomed
or shrieked or splashed.

All was still. Including the flying carpet.

Wilbur jumped onto Winnie's shoulder.
'Purr, purr,' he said.

Then Winnie rolled up the flying carpet.
'Let's go home, Wilbur,' she said.
'By broomstick!'

Winnie waved her magic wand backwards.

'Abracadabra!'

she shouted, and everything started again.

Wheee! Zooom! Whizzzz! Vroom!

Winnie and Wilbur landed in Winnie's garden.
Winnie frowned at the flying carpet.

What would she do with it?

Then Winnie had a wonderful idea.
She shut her eyes,
waved her wand, shouted,

. . . and there, tied to two trees,
was a beautiful hammock.

Winnie and Wilbur climbed in.
They were both very tired.

The hammock rocked gently
in the breeze.

'This is so comfortable, Wilbur,'
said Winnie.

But Wilbur didn't hear her.
He was already fast asleep.

Winnie and Wilbur
THE AMAZING PUMPKIN

Winnie the Witch ate lots of vegetables.

She liked broccoli, cauliflower,
cabbage, and parsnips.
She really liked peas, carrots,
beans, potatoes, and spinach.

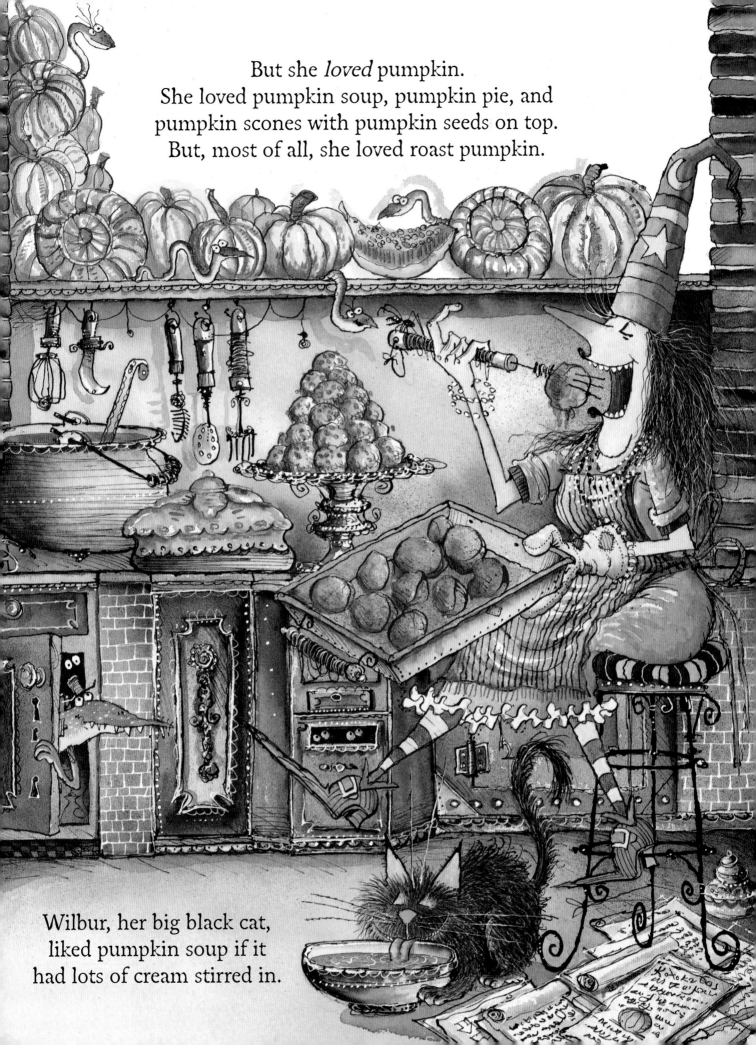

But she *loved* pumpkin.
She loved pumpkin soup, pumpkin pie, and
pumpkin scones with pumpkin seeds on top.
But, most of all, she loved roast pumpkin.

Wilbur, her big black cat,
liked pumpkin soup if it
had lots of cream stirred in.

Every Saturday morning Winnie
would jump onto her broomstick,
Wilbur would jump onto her
shoulder, and they would zoom
off to the farmers' market
to buy their vegetables.

That was easy.

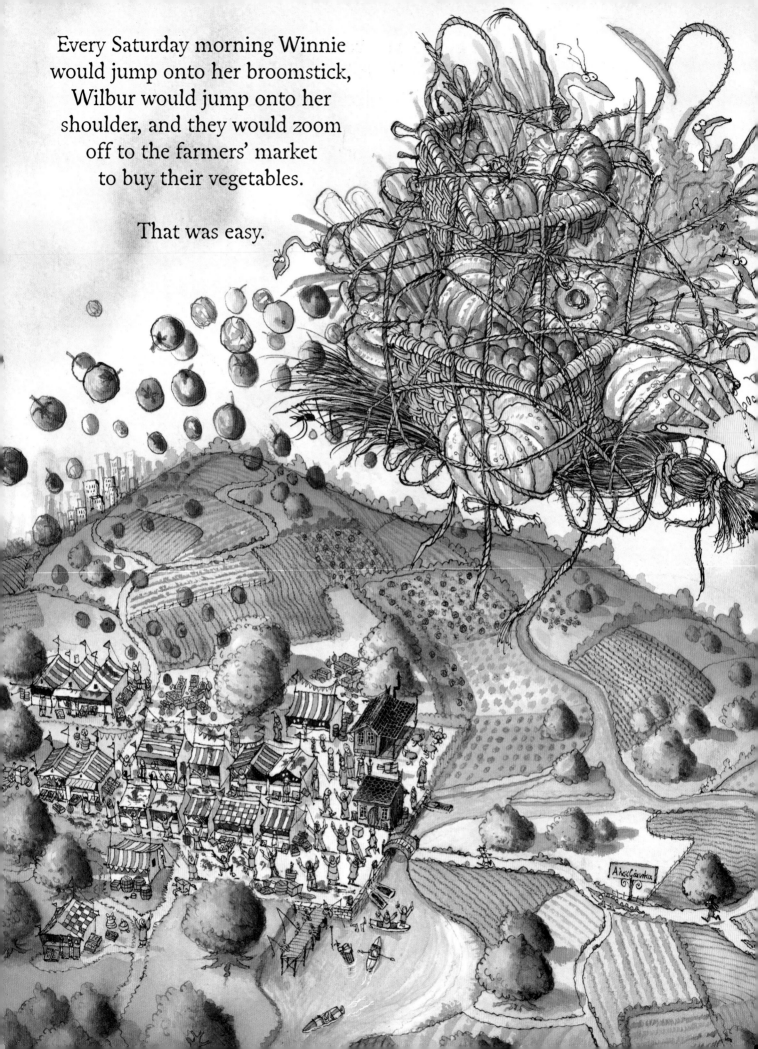

But it wasn't so easy coming home.
It is hard to balance on a broomstick with
a cat, pumpkins, and lots of other vegetables.

Ooops! Brussels sprouts and tomatoes
rained down on the market.

Splat! Squelch!

'Blithering broomsticks!' shouted Winnie.
And then she had a good idea.

'I'll grow my own vegetables,' she said.
So Winnie dug a big vegetable patch
in her garden.

Wilbur helped.

She planted lots and lots of vegetables.
She watered the plants and pulled up
the weeds.

Wilbur helped.

But the plants grew very slowly.

And, when they did grow, the caterpillars
and snails and rabbits ate them.

'Oh dear,' said Winnie. 'Gardening is hard work.
I'll try a spell to help my garden grow.'

She waved her magic wand, shouted,

'Abracadabra!'

and nothing happened.

'Bother!' said Winnie.
'That didn't work.
I'll go and look in my
Big Book of Spells.'

Winnie went inside
just a minute too soon.

Outside, the spell
began to work.

Inside, it was very dark.
Winnie tripped over Wilbur.
'Meooowww!'
'I'm sorry, Wilbur,' said Winnie,
'I didn't see you. It's so dark, there
must be a storm on the way.'

She looked out of the window.
It wasn't a storm.
It was Winnie's garden.
The vegetables were growing so fast
they covered all the windows.

'I'd better go out and stop
the spell,' Winnie said.

But the door wouldn't open.
An enormous cabbage was in the way.

Winnie rushed upstairs, climbed
out of the bathroom window,
and slid down a giant beanstalk.

Wilbur climbed down behind her.
This is fun! he thought,
until he met a giant caterpillar.
'Yeeoow!'

Everything in Winnie's garden was
enormous, gigantic, stupendous!

A beanstalk was growing up into the clouds.
The cabbages were as big as cows.
The rabbits were bigger than cows.
An immense pumpkin vine was curling
around Winnie's house.

And there, on the roof, was a **huge** pumpkin.
'Oh no!' shouted Winnie.
'The pumpkin will squash my house!'
She waved her magic wand,
but just as she shouted . . .

'Abra . . .

CRASH!

... cadabra!'

the gigantic pumpkin
crashed to the ground.

Winnie's enormous, stupendous garden
shrank back to the way it was before.

But the pumpkin that had broken
off the vine was still a massive,
monstrous, amazing pumpkin.

Winnie chopped a doorway into the pumpkin.

She made pumpkin pies, pumpkin scones,
pumpkin soup with cream for Wilbur, and
an enormous dish of roast pumpkin.

But there was still lots of pumpkin left.

So she put a notice on the gate:

FREE PUMPKIN
Help yourself...

People came with their bowls and
baskets and even wheelbarrows.

And soon the pumpkin shell was empty.

'What shall I do with the pumpkin shell?' wondered Winnie.
'It would make a good house, but I already have a house.

One of my friends once changed a pumpkin into a coach.
But that was for a special occasion.
And the horses might be a problem.'

Then Winnie had a wonderful idea.
'Yes!' she said. 'That's exactly what
it looks like,' she said. 'Of course!'

She waved her magic wand,
stamped her foot, shouted,

'Abracadabra!'

and there, in Winnie's garden,
was a bright orange helicopter.

So now, when Winnie and Wilbur go to the market, Winnie can buy as many pumpkins as she likes.

And flying home in a helicopter is lots of fun!

OXFORD
UNIVERSITY PRESS

Great Clarendon Street, Oxford OX2 6DP

Oxford University Press is a department of the University of Oxford. It furthers the University's objective of excellence in research, scholarship, and education by publishing worldwide. Oxford is a registered trade mark of Oxford University Press in the UK and in certain other countries

Text copyright © Valerie Thomas 1999, 2008, 2009
Illustrations copyright © Korky Paul 1999, 2008, 2009, 2016, 2017
The moral rights of the author and artist have been asserted

Database right Oxford University Press (maker)

Winnie and Wilbur: The Broomstick Ride first published as Winnie Flies Again in 1999
Winnie and Wilbur: The Flying Carpet first published as Winnie's Flying Carpet in 2008
Winnie and Wilbur: The Amazing Pumpkin first published as Winnie's Amazing Pumpkin in 2009
Winnie and Wilbur: Up, Up and Away first published in 2017

The stories are complete and unabridged

British Library Cataloguing in Publication Data available

ISBN: 978-0-19-275894-1

10 9 8 7 6 5 4 3 2 1

Printed in China

Paper used in the production of this book is a natural, recyclable product made from wood grown in sustainable forests. The manufacturing process conforms to the environmental regulations of the country of origin

www.winnieandwilbur.com

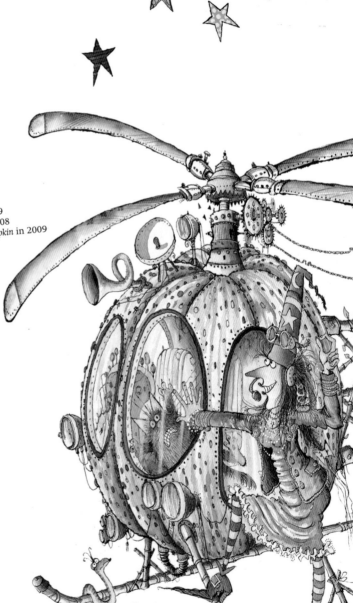